Fairythorn Tales

by Lara Faraway

Rose and the Friendship Wish

templar

A TEMPLAR BOOK

First published in the UK in 2013

by Templar Publishing,

an imprint of The Templar Company Limited,

Deepdene Lodge, Deepdene Avenue,

Dorking, Surrey,

RH5 4AT, UK

www.templarco.co.uk

Text by Sara Starbuck
Illustrations by Jan McCafferty
Design copyright © 2013 The Templar Company Ltd
Scents copyright © Celessence

ISBN 978 1 84877 968 6

Printed and bound in Great Britain by
CPI Group (UK) Ltd, Croydon, CR0 4YY

Prologue

Our world is only the beginning. Beneath the surface and between the moonbeams there is another place. A place where the flowers sing and birds and animals live happily with the little people of Fairyland.

All the magic in our world comes from this place, through doorways that only the fairies can open. And, at the centre of the magic is the Fairythorn Tree.

The Fairythorn, as the little people call it, is always the oldest tree in any garden, wood or park. It might be gnarled and spiky on the outside, but it is a comfortable home for the tiny fairies who live hidden inside its trunk and branches.

And if you look very closely, right down where the base of the trunk meets the mossy ground, you might just spot a doorway to the fairies' world.

Look very closely, now. It's even smaller than you think…

Chapter 1

In a patch of trees at the bottom of a scruffy garden, magic was happening. This was quite normal here, because one of the trees was a fairythorn and fairythorns always mean magic.

Wishes, spells and tiny flying things were busily bashing into each other in the air. The garden's birds were noisily tuning their voices. Even the spiders were competing to spin the most spectacular web of the day.

Everyone was busy, except for four tiny fairies sitting on the highest branch of the Fairythorn Tree. Their pale-green draglings, the magical companions of all fairies, hovered above them. The tiny dragon-like creatures were making little mewls that were cute, in a scratchy sort of a way.

Three of the fairies, Posy, Fleur and Honeysuckle, were watching their dragling friends happily, but the fourth fairy, Rose, looked worried. She sat in the middle of the branch, twiddling one of her long brown plaits between her fingers.

"Are you sure we've got time for a race?" Rose asked as she tightened the straps of the pink parachute draped over her back. The parachute was made from an old silk hanky that one of the Bigs had dropped last winter. Hankies were getting rarer and rarer these days, so Rose had been delighted to find it. The silk had come in handy already – so far she had made three pretty dresses out of it, as well as the parachute.

She looked down the branch at the others with a serious expression on her face. "Mother Nature said she wanted us all in our places for the May Day celebrations by morning. And listen…"

All four of them cupped their pointy ears and listened to the sun rising. To fairies, dawn sounds a bit like an orchestra tuning up.

"Course we've got time, silly,"

grinned Posy, her green eyes sparkling with mischief and delight. "Can't you hear it? The day's miles off yet. The sunrise fairies have only just got going. You're such a worrywart, Rose."

Posy adjusted the feather headdress in her hair. "Anyway," she sniffed, "it won't take me long to win."

"Oi!" said Fleur. She tossed back her fiery red hair, leaving a trail of little silver sparks in the air around her head. "Don't be so sure about that!" Fleur stood up on the branch and bent over to strap a wide leaf to her feet. It looked like a curled green surfboard.

She grinned at her dragling, Red, who swooped down to lick her on the nose. "Me and Red have been practising," she said with a wink.

Rose frowned thoughtfully. Posy was right, there was loads of time before the day's business began. She just hated letting anybody down, especially if that anybody was Mother Nature. But they could have their race and still get back to the Fairythorn

Tree in plenty of time for the start of the celebrations.

Rose got up, breathing in the early morning air. It was going to be a beautiful day. Her dragling, Pax, broke away from her play-fight with the other draglings to nuzzle against Rose's neck, before mewling cheerfully and flapping away again.

"All right then," Rose said. "May the best fairy win."

"That's the spirit," said Honeysuckle. The tiny bells in her golden hair jingled as she jumped to her feet and stepped onto the nearest sunbeam. She bounced up and down gently to test it for strength and springiness. "Does everyone remember the rules?"

"Get to the Bigs' house as quickly as possible, by any means necessary," said Rose, pointing over at the large, slightly shabby house at the other end of the garden. It was the place where the humans lived. "Is everyone ready?"

"Hang on," said Posy, sticking her fingers in her mouth and giving a shrill whistle. Suddenly a sleek, blue swallow swept down onto the branch beside her and the draglings were sent

spinning. They growled and snapped but the bird just ignored them. Posy hopped on to the swallow's back and stroked its glossy feathers encouragingly.

"I think we're all ready now, Rose!" Posy said. "On your marks, get set... GO!"

Chapter 2

In a blast of multi-coloured sparks, the fairies launched themselves from the top of the tree. Their draglings followed close behind, growling with excitement.

Rose took a flying leap, throwing herself as far from the branch as she could. As she dropped, the pink silk parachute filled with air and she slowly floated towards the ground.

Honeysuckle sat down on her

sunbeam and began
to slide. Her long
hair flew out
behind her like
a golden cape.

Posy and
her swallow
shot skywards before
turning and plunging back towards the
earth like an upside-down firework.

And, surfing down the branches
on her leaf board, came Fleur, riding
the bumps of the Fairythorn Tree as
if they were waves on the sea.

The race was on!

Rose knew she was bound to come in last, as usual, but she didn't mind. She was just so happy it was May Day at last! Rose had been looking forward to it for ages. May Day was like all the special days in the human world rolled into one, coated in chocolate and dipped in sprinkles.

On May Day, the doors of fairyland were always swung wide open, so that Mother Nature's magic could pour out to help the natural world come back to life. It was the most powerful, magical day of the year, and it made Rose shiver with delight just thinking about it.

Rose waved at her friend Buttercup, who was balancing on a fairythorn branch, polishing the leaves to a deep green shine. The rest of the fairies and garden creatures had stopped to watch too. The four friends were always racing and their antics usually drew a crowd.

"Come on, Rose," shouted Buttercup from her branch. "Don't let Posy win again."

Out in the lead, Posy was almost at the Bigs' house already. Honeysuckle was close behind on her early morning

sunbeam. Fleur was halfway across
the garden, where she'd dumped her
leaf board and jumped on the back
of a wood mouse. She was holding its
ears like the reins of a horse and the
mouse looked quite grumpy about it.

As Rose floated lazily towards
the ground a bright flash of brilliant

blue and apple-green caught her eye. She turned her head to see a dragonfly hovering beside her, buzzing enthusiastically.

"Thanks," said Rose. "I suppose I would get there faster if I let you take me…" She slid onto the dragonfly's back and wriggled out of the parachute straps. The scrap of pink silk drifted to the ground. Rose held tight and the dragonfly let rip!

As they sped towards the house, Rose spotted a little girl staring out of a bedroom window. *She must be one of the new family of Bigs who arrived*

a week ago, Rose
thought.

The little girl
had long, mousy
brown hair and a sad
look on her face.

Rose was just
pondering what might
make a little Big feel
sad, when there was
a scream. She glanced down just in
time to see Honeysuckle shooting off
the end of her sunbeam.

Honeysuckle landed with an
uncomfortable thump in a patch of

daisies. The little fairy sneezed and a cloud of golden daisy pollen puffed out around her.

By chance, Honeysuckle had landed right next to the Bigs' back door. Posy swept down after her, jumped off the swallow and yelled a quick "thank you" over her shoulder.

Rose and the dragonfly arrived seconds later, reaching the back door at the same time as Fleur and her field mouse. All four draglings swooped down to sit at their fairy's ankles, like obedient puppies.

"Well done, you win," said Posy,

shaking Honeysuckle's hand.

"Yes, but look," said Honeysuckle miserably, pointing at the daisies. "I broke three stems. I've properly crushed them." Her dragling, Pip, fluttered up to curl around her neck as tears filled her bright-blue eyes. "We're meant to look after living things, not crash-land on them. What's Mother Nature going to say?"

Rose climbed off the dragonfly and walked over to give her friend a hug.

"Mother Nature will know it was an accident," Rose said warmly. "And anyway, daisies are tougher than they look. They'll bounce back. Bet you anything."

Honeysuckle shook her head furiously. Tears were rolling down her cheeks now. "What if she's cross?" she sobbed. "What if she won't let me go to the Spring Ball?"

Fleur gasped in horror and clapped a hand over her mouth. "No fairy should ever miss the Spring Ball," she said. "Maybe Mother Nature didn't see you?"

"No chance, Fleur," said Posy. "Mother Nature sees and knows everything, so how could she possibly miss this? I guess we'll find out what she has to say about it soon enough."

But Fleur wasn't listening any more. She was staring over Posy's shoulder at the Fairythorn Tree in the distance. The wind had picked up and the leaves were whispering to each other. All four fairies watched as the tree began to shimmer and shine. Honeysuckle nervously scrambled behind a dandelion leaf. The doorway was opening. Mother Nature had arrived.

Chapter 3

Rose and her friends had to get back to the Fairythorn Tree, fast. Posy startled a passing blackbird with a sharp, shrill whistle. The bird swept down and the fairies clambered onto her warm feathery back.

"Hurry up," Posy shouted to Rose, "I don't want us to get into worse trouble than we are already."

"That's not fairily possible," said Rose.

"Don't you believe it," Posy answered. "You know how Mother Nature feels about lateness."

"Well budge up then," said Rose. "You've only left me the tail feathers to hang on to. And anyway..." she added. "It was me who warned you lot that we didn't have time for a race. Remember?"

"I wish I'd listened," Honeysuckle whispered. "Then I wouldn't have flattened those daisies."

The fairies wriggled up the blackbird's back to make some room, and Rose hopped on. Their draglings hovered beside them like impatient drivers waiting for the lights to change.

The first note of morning sounded just as the sparrow took to the air. To fairy ears, it was the sweetest, most beautiful sound in the world. But Rose could only squeak in horror and tighten her grip around Posy's waist.

"We're not going to make it," she wailed. "We're doomed!"

"We'll make it," said Fleur confidently. "We're only a flip and a flap away."

But a golden ball of light had already started to appear just in front of the Fairythorn Tree. It hung in the air like the glow from an invisible candle. Then it grew larger, and as it grew, a single, snow-white butterfly fluttered out from its centre. Then another butterfly appeared. Blue this time. Then a purple one, then red, then pink, orange and indigo... In one great whoosh, a whole rainbow of butterflies burst out of the strange ball of light and filled the space under the tree.

"Quick!" said Rose, as the blackbird came in to land on one of the Fairythorn's branches. "Everyone into position."

Now that she was standing with all the other fairies ready for Mother Nature's visit, Rose was starting to relax again. She allowed herself a little shiver of excitement and pride as she looked around at her home.

The tree was at its most beautiful. Every branch was lined with the fairies who lived there. There were hundreds of them. All of the fairies had made sure to look their very best for Mother Nature's May Day celebrations. There were wildflower crowns and dewdrop earrings, fancy feather headbands and dresses spun from spider silk or made from the Bigs' discarded treasures.

One little fairy had made a very pretty party dress from a scrap of tinfoil, with holes at the back for her delicate, shimmering dragonfly wings.

"This is it," whispered Posy excitedly, fishing a leaf out of Honeysuckle's tangled hair.

The Fairy Chorus had started singing along with the sunrise and the chattering birds. The golden light that hung under the Fairythorn Tree shone especially bright for a moment, like a second sun. And then from the very heart of it stepped a young woman. At first she seemed to be made from nothing but sunbeams and dandelion seeds blown on the wind. But then everything fell into place. She was beautiful, with sea-green eyes, milk-white skin and hair the colour of autumn leaves, tied up in a crown of flowers. It was Mother Nature.

"Hello my fairy friends," she called in a voice that was both loud and clear, soft and soothing. "Thank you for joining me on this most important day."

There was a cheer from the crowd. Mother Nature picked a different tree every year to visit on May Day and it was a huge honour to have your tree chosen.

"There will be time to celebrate at the Spring Ball this evening, but for now there is work to be done," said Mother Nature, smiling. "I'm sure the Bigs think that the world takes care of itself. But we know better. Every one of you is destined for your own special job here. Some of you have already found your purpose and your wings have unfurled, and some of you are yet to discover it. But every single job is important, and I thank you all for the hard work that you do."

The fairies clapped, proudly.

Mother Nature went on, "Today is the day we must work our hardest. The winter has been long, but now it's time to wake up the world."

She stepped to one side of the golden light and let the magic from fairyland flow into the world like a gushing tap. As it touched the trees, clouds of pink and white blossom burst into life.

"You young fairies who don't know your jobs yet, please help out wherever you can," said Mother Nature. "If you're unsure, then ask.

You'll find me… well," she paused and smiled. "You'll find me everywhere. Just call." She clapped her hands and there was a bustle of activity as the fairies scampered off to their duties.

"Not you four," she added sternly, beckoning to Rose and her friends as they turned to leave. "I think we need to have a little chat…"

Chapter 4

"I'm so sorry," said Honeysuckle. Her eyes were full of tears and her bottom lip was wobbling. "Fairy's honour, I didn't mean to hurt those daisies."

"I know you didn't," said Mother Nature. "You never do. But this sort of thing keeps happening, Honeysuckle, and I simply can't have careless fairies working in the Bigs' world." She arched an eyebrow. "There are plenty in Fairyland who would give their wings for your place here."

Honeysuckle gasped at the thought of being sent back to live in Fairyland and leaving her friends behind.

Rose was lined up silently with the others in front of Mother Nature. She reached out and squeezed her friend's hand gently. Rose understood completely. Fairyland was wonderful, of course, but there was something special about where the Bigs lived. In Fairyland, everything was magical, but the Bigs' world was like a funfair, packed full of mystery and wonder.

There was a burst of noise as the gang's draglings sped past, chasing a poppy seed that was caught on the breeze. Some of the other fairies stopped working to see what was going on, but a glance from Mother Nature and they were all busy with their tasks again.

"I will try harder," Honeysuckle

said, "I promise! Please, please, please, don't send me back to live in Fairyland." Her cheeks were pink and her eyes were filling with tears. "I'll never have another race again if you tell me not to." She gulped back a sob. "Or have any fun at all."

"Don't be silly, Honeysuckle," said Mother Nature, her face softening. "It's simply a case of looking where you're going." She waved a hand. "Your races are fine, as long as your work is done first. But try not to crash about so. You really must be more careful."

"I really will be… really," said

Honeysuckle, picking at the hem of her skirt nervously. "I really, really—"

Honeysuckle was cut short as a procession of worker ants marched straight between her and Mother Nature, laden with food for the evening's feast.

It was well known in the Fairythorn Tree that ants take their work very seriously. And for that reason, they were a popular method of fairy luggage transport. All the fairies had to do was make sure they knew where the ants were going, then pop their bags on the ants' backs.

A worker ant would always get a fairy's luggage to its destination by the shortest route possible.

The leaves and berries that these worker ants carried on their backs were bigger than the ants themselves, and Honeysuckle and her friends had to move back to get out of the way as they tramped past.

When the procession had passed by, Mother Nature sat down and patted the ground for the fairies to join her. A thick circle of daisies and buttercups immediately sprang up around them.

Rose looked at Honeysuckle's worried face. She hated it when anyone felt bad and always tried to help.

"Excuse me, Mother Nature," she said, blushing and sitting up a bit straighter. "Honeysuckle and I had a bet about whether sunbeams were faster than flower hopping. So really, this is all my fault."

"No!" said Fleur, folding her arms across her chest. "The race was my idea, so it's my fault."

Posy shook her head so hard that her feathered headdress wobbled like a startled turkey.

"Honeysuckle only took the sunbeam because she knew I'd beat her otherwise," she said, bursting into a grin. "As always."

Honeysuckle flashed a grateful smile at her friends before turning back to face Mother Nature.

"They all know it's my fault really," she said, miserably. "And I really am very sorry."

Mother Nature looked from fairy to fairy. They wriggled uncomfortably as they waited for another telling off.

"Fairies," Mother Nature said at last, "I don't expect you to shy away from adventure, but do try to remember why you are here. You are Nature's guardians and must be careful to protect and respect the natural world around you, from the tallest tree to the tiniest bloom. Leave the destruction to the Grot Goblins."

Mother Nature's eyes darkened to the colour of a stormy sea. They narrowed as she peered into the gloomiest corner of the garden.

"You'll all have noticed that

the grease and the muck are getting worse," she said, wrinkling her nose. "The Grot Goblins' footprints are all over the world now. They thrive on the grime that the Bigs' machines belch out."

"There are loads of slugs too," said Posy. "You can always tell when Grot Goblins have been here. They're like slug magnets!"

Rose shivered. She'd never seen a Grot Goblin — not many fairies had. But she knew all the terrifying stories, and she'd seen the damage they left behind. Grot Goblins hated the natural world just as much as fairies loved it.

"So you see the battle we have on our hands," Mother Nature continued. "They're destroying everything." She paused and sighed. "But, today isn't about all that." She flapped her hands, like she was trying to wave the problem away. "It's the first day of spring. Today we celebrate."

"So… um… am I still in trouble?" asked Honeysuckle, shyly.

"Can she still come to the Spring Ball?" Fleur added.

Mother Nature smiled. "No and yes," she said. "In that order."

Fleur thought about that for a moment and then let out a little whoop. Honeysuckle let out the breath that she'd been holding.

"Do remember to slow down though, Honeysuckle," Mother Nature warned again. "You're a fairy, not a mini tornado."

She stood up, pollen falling from her skirt, and smiled broadly. "Right then," she said briskly. "Work hard. I'll see you all later."

Rose and her friends watched

as Mother Nature wandered off to talk to a group of squirrels. As she went, she bent low and swept a hand over the bare ground. A bright patch of bluebells sprang to life where her fingers touched the soil.

"Phew, that was a close one," said Honeysuckle, sighing with relief.

"Remind me never to race on a sunbeam again."

"Okay," said Posy, cheerfully. "Especially as that will mean you'll definitely never beat me again."

By now the sun was higher in the sky and the dewdrops were sparkling like little diamonds. Rose grinned at her friends and clapped her hands. "Come on," she said. "It's going to be a beautiful day."

As they skipped off to work, none of the fairies realised that they were being watched from the window of the Bigs' house. Indeed, Alice, whose window it was, couldn't be sure herself that she had seen anything in particular, more than the rustle of the wind in the shaggy lawn. But for a moment, she was certain there was something unusual out there in the garden. A strange glow. The shape of a person. A cluster of tiny, sparkling… somethings.

"I need to go to bed earlier," said Alice, rubbing her eyes. She turned away from the window and headed downstairs for breakfast.

Chapter 5

"Oi, midgets, keep your pets under control," said an angry voice from the back of the garden.

"Some of us are trying to have an argument over here," yelled another cross-sounding voice.

Rose groaned. The shouting could only be coming from Derek and Clive, the grouchiest garden gnomes known to fairykind.

Derek and Clive were sitting

next to the small pond at the bottom of the garden. They were identical gnomes, with red pointy hats, long white beards, blue tunics and grumpy faces. The only way to tell them apart was by the crack in Clive's concrete hat, or by the awful names they called each other.

"Weren't they over by the fence yesterday?" asked Rose, looking from one end of the garden to the other with confusion. "How do they get around? They're only garden ornaments!"

"Shouting garden ornaments," said Posy. "They got accidentally zapped with Mother Nature's magic last time she was here, remember?" She turned and pointed to a small apple tree near the house. "They were over there before they turned up by the fence."

"Isn't it a bit weird that no one's ever actually seen them move?" said Rose.

"Oi, Stinkerbell," roared Clive, "Your dragling's just pooped on my fishing rod!"

Fleur gasped. "Stinkerbell?" she

spluttered. "I ought to go over there with a hammer. Then we'd see if they can move."

Honeysuckle burst out laughing. "Let them grumble," she said. "They're rude, but they're no trouble really. And don't worry, they can't walk or anything. The Bigs have been arguing about where to put them. They're just trying out different positions."

There was a high-pitched wail and the fairies turned to see their draglings dive-bombing

Derek with clods of mud.

"See?" said Honeysuckle. "You'd move out of the way of that if you could!"

"I suppose we'd better rescue them," grinned Posy.

"Do we have to?" asked Fleur, mischievously. "It looks like the draglings are having fun." But her eyes suddenly widened as she watched her dragling, Red, puff a jet of green fairy fire at Derek's beard.

"HOT! HOT! HOT!" screamed Derek. "Get this fluffy lizardling away from me!"

Fleur stuck her fingers in her mouth and gave three short, shrill whistles. Red flew to her side obediently.

"Bad boy, Red!" said Fleur firmly, as her dragling skidded to a halt on the grass at her feet. "Don't set fire to the grumpy gnomes."

"They're made of concrete," said Posy. "You can't set fire to them. I suppose their paint might bubble up a bit though."

Red looked up at his fairy with impossibly wide eyes and mewed sweetly. Fleur's stern face immediately gave way to a smile. She kneeled down and threw her arms around his neck.

"You mustn't use your fire like that," Fleur whispered. "Especially when Mother Nature is around."

Posy's dragling, Dash, flapped over to join his fairy, with Pax and Pip following close behind.

"Sooner or later," Rose warned the chattering draglings, "those gnomes will find a way to get even with you for teasing them."

She bent down to scoop Pax up in her arms. "Stop winding them up, even if they are awful, or you might regret it."

None of the draglings looked particularly worried.

Chapter 6

Before long, Rose and her friends had found ways to be helpful. Posy had fluttered off on a butterfly to help the pollen spreaders. A big brown toad had hopped by to collect Fleur for lily-pad polishing duty. Honeysuckle was busy organising the bees, who would happily sit at home all day eating honey if the fairies weren't there to nudge them out the door every morning.

None of them knew their special

job yet, but they were looking forward to finding out. Especially because they knew that when a fairy discovers her job, her wings unfurl. Fairies who live by water might have shimmering wings like a dragonfly. Fairies who live in woodlands might have feathery wings like birds, or wings shaped like oak leaves. Rose couldn't wait to find out what hers would look like.

Rose was going to search for decorations for the ball, and she'd been waiting for a wood mouse to give her a lift.

"Thanks very much for the ride,"

said Rose, as a mouse stopped to let her hop on its back.

"Come on, Pax," she called out eagerly. "I saw something shiny over by the shed earlier. Let's check it out."

Pax had been stretched out on an open flower, sunbathing. She jumped up at Rose's call and tumbled through the air towards her, mewling excitedly. Draglings love shiny things as much as fairies do.

Rose was about to stroke the mouse's ears to signal she was ready to go, then something stopped her in her tracks. With all the busyness, nobody had noticed a little girl standing by the Fairythorn Tree. She seemed to be talking to the tree trunk.

"Pax, look!" Rose whispered. "It's the little Big from earlier." She edged her mouse forwards as quietly as possible, until she could hear what the Big was saying.

Rose looked around for Mother Nature, but she was nowhere to be seen. Most of the other fairies were either inside the tree preparing for the ball or off working in the garden.

"So you see," the girl was saying, "I haven't made any friends yet. We've been here a whole month already and I've still got nobody to play with."

She sighed deeply and kicked a pebble with the toe of her trainer. It shot off in Rose's direction, missing her by a whisker.

"Mum and Dad are too busy and tired to help, and I'm really lonely." She looked down at the ground sadly. "Sometimes I think I might be invisible."

No wonder she looks so sad, thought Rose.

The little girl pulled a small pink ribbon out of her pocket and started to wrap it around the lowest branch of the Fairythorn Tree. Pink was Rose's favourite colour.

"My granny says if you tie a ribbon to a fairy tree on May Day, the fairies who live there might like it and grant your wish," the little girl said. She tied the ends of the ribbon into a neat bow. "So, fairies, if you're listening, my name's Alice, this is my favourite ribbon and I hope you like it as much as I do."

Alice stepped back from the tree and closed her eyes tight. "Please help me to find a new friend."

"Oh dear," said Rose, watching Alice and shaking her head. "This won't do. It won't do at all!"

Rose was sad that the little Big was lonely, but at that moment she was more worried that Alice was standing very VERY close to the doorway that led to Fairyland.

On any other day, this wouldn't

matter one bit. For fairies, passing between their realm and the Bigs' world is a simple matter of making a wish. But for humans, a trip to Fairyland would take some serious magic. Except on May Day, when the doors to Fairyland are left wide open for Mother Nature's magic to pour through. Should a Big happen to make a wish by the open door of a Fairythorn on this day, there's a good chance they will be swept up in all the fast-flowing magic and whisked away to Fairyland.

And that means serious trouble...

Chapter 7

Alice was on the move. She was pacing back and forth in front of the Fairythorn Tree, the toes of her trainers almost touching the tiny hidden doorway.

"Oh, goblin guts," Rose muttered. She slid off the mouse's back and stood with her hands on her hips, thinking.

"The little Big's going to get sucked in, Pax," said Rose. "We have to do something."

Pax flopped down beside her on the grass and made a noise a bit like a baby goat, which was sweet but not particularly helpful.

"We're going to have to get her away from the tree somehow," said Rose. She looked around, thinking hard. Then an idea came to her. It was risky, but it was her only chance. She whistled softly to a passing sparrow, who fluttered down to land beside her. Rose hopped onto its back.

"Up, friend," she said, "and fast, please!"

The sparrow took off at once,

with Pax following close behind, growling with excitement.

Alice had stopped right in front of the threshold to Fairyland. The door was belching out great waves of fairy magic, then sucking them back in again, like the ebb and flow of the sea. Tendrils of magic were coiling around Alice's feet. The fairy realm wanted Alice and her wish.

"Please hurry," said Rose to the sparrow, "we haven't got much time." She pointed in the direction of the wooden shed. The sparrow flapped hard and darted over to the little tumbledown building.

"It's down there," said Rose, pointing to a shiny sweet wrapper. "Under the lavender bush." She turned to her dragling. "Pax! Fetch!"

Pax dived straight down and snatched up the wrapper in her teeth. She launched herself up again, like a rocket, straight back to Rose and the sparrow hovering above the shed roof.

"Well done, Pax," said Rose, grabbing the

wrapper. "Now, you need to stay here while I go and distract that Big. There's no time to lose."

Alice had started pacing again. Long wisps of fairy magic were now creeping up towards her knees.

"Oh no!" cried Rose, "It's happening!" The magic was twisting about Alice faster now, knotting itself around her.

"Quickly!" Rose commanded the sparrow, "Put us right in front of her. Right under her nose."

The magic was curling around Alice's waist now, and still the little

Big hadn't noticed. The sparrow got into position and Rose lifted the shiny wrapper over her head, waggling it about. Sunlight bounced off the foil and the dazzle caught Alice's eye. She stared open-mouthed at the odd bird, and the tiny, shiny thing on its back. Her eyes widened with excitement.

"I knew it," Alice cried, clapping her hands to her face. "I knew fairies were real."

"Whoops," said Rose.

Rose knew that what she had done was incredibly risky. One of Mother Nature's golden rules was that fairies should never let the Bigs see them. But there wasn't time to worry about that. A few moments more and Alice would be sucked into Fairyland for ever.

"We have to lead her away," Rose said to the sparrow.

The sparrow turned in the air and started to fly away from the tree.

"Hey, hang on," said Alice, turning to run after them. The glowing tendrils of magic slipped and slid away from her body as she left the doorway behind her.

Rose breathed a sigh of relief

and directed the sparrow towards the Bigs' house.

"Please don't go!" Alice cried out as she jogged after them. "I just want someone to be friends with me."

But as much as Rose wanted to stop and talk to the lonely little girl, she knew it was forbidden. So, with a heavy heart, she sent the sparrow soaring upwards and out of sight, leaving Alice by her back door with a very sad look on her face.

Chapter 8

By early evening the Spring Ball was in full swing. Mother Nature had sown a ring of plump toadstools around the Fairythorn Tree and cast a spell that made everything inside the ring invisible, except for the tree itself. A Big would have to step right inside the ring to see the fairies.

The sky was a deep red and the fairies of the Sunset Choir were singing at the tops of their voices. All fairies can sing, but the fairies in the choir sing so beautifully that humans mistake them for songbirds.

Inside the ring of toadstools some fairies were dancing and others were talking or tucking into the feast. Those with wings had groomed them with extra care. Some were sprinkled with moondust for extra sparkle, or decorated with broken bits of star, or polished with a balm made from glow-worm silk and cinnamon bark.

There were draglings all over the place, too – tumbling through the air and chasing each other between the stalks of the toadstools.

Mother Nature sat elegantly among them all, singing along with the Sunset Choir. Colourful butterflies had settled in her hair like living hair clips and dozens of other creatures had come into the circle, just to be close to her. A litter of baby ladybirds was curled up in her lap. A dormouse had settled down next to her, snoring gently.

And a snoozy barn owl, who had just woken up from his day's sleep, was perched above her in the Fairythorn Tree, hooting happily.

The tree itself looked spectacular, with glossy green leaves and big clusters of sweet-smelling white blossom. The fairies had decorated it with all the pretty things they could find.

There were brightly coloured ribbons dangling from the branches, along with the pink one that Alice had left behind. There were shiny shards of old CDs and sparkling slivers of coloured glass. A string of red berries had been wrapped around the trunk, and there, fluttering on a thorn on a low branch, was Rose's silver wrapper – the one she'd used to get Alice's attention.

"Are you absolutely sure the little Big saw you?" Honeysuckle asked.

Rose nodded. "As sure as I can see you," she mumbled miserably, sinking her face into her hands.

Posy put an arm around her friend and gave her a squeeze.

"Don't be upset, Rose. I'm sure it will be fine," she said gently. "You were only trying to help, after all."

Rose peeped through her fingers.

"But I still broke Rule Number One of the Fairy Code," she said. "If the Bigs find out about us it will ruin everything."

"I think you were really brave," said Fleur. "You couldn't just let

the little Big get dragged away to Fairyland. Don't really see what else you could've done."

"Fleur's right," said Honeysuckle. "We're the guardians of the doorway. It's our job not to let any Bigs through."

"Even little Bigs," Fleur added.

"But Alice saw me," said Rose, fiddling with a flower in her hair. "What am I going to tell Mother Nature?"

At that moment, on the far side of the circle, Mother Nature turned and looked directly at Rose. She smiled and winked.

"I think she might already know," gasped Honeysuckle.

"Of course she knows," said Posy. "She probably knew before you did, Rose."

Rose relaxed a bit. Mother Nature didn't seem to be cross.

"But what do we do about the Bigs?" she said, frowning.

"Children see fairies all the time." said Fleur. "The grown-up Bigs always tell them it's their imagination. After a while the children actually believe the grown-ups. That's how we've stayed hidden for so long."

Rose looked around at her friends' kind faces and smiled brightly. She didn't want her worries to ruin their evening. "You're right," she said. "I'm sure Alice will have forgotten all about me by the morning."

But Rose couldn't get the little Big and her sad face out of her head.

Honeysuckle stood up, the dancing had begun and she was eager to join in. She held out her hands to her friends and they all clambered to their feet.

They were just about to start a jig when the music was interrupted by a flash of bright light and a familiar sound, like the ringing of a thousand tiny bells. A loud cheer rang out as one young fairy jumped to her feet in a shower of golden sparks, and everyone watched as her wings began to unfurl.

Rose recognised the fairy at once. It was her friend Flicker. Flicker's wings were a soft, velvety black, with bright red bands across them and white spots. Just like a Red Admiral butterfly, Rose realised. Flicker's dragling, Fizz, was changing too, his scales turning the same colours as his fairy's new wings.

"Congratulations
Flicker," Mother
Nature called over.
"Congratulations,
Fizz. Flicker, you
are a Pollen Fairy,
which is a good thing
as the butterflies and
bees need all the help they
can get this year. And both of you
look quite magnificent."

Flicker beamed with pride and
beat her new wings until her feet left

the ground. She floated on the spot, scattering fairy dust with every flap.

Honeysuckle flopped back down on the floor again.

"I'll never get my wings," she sighed, twisting her arm to touch the little curled nubs on her back. They were like flower buds ready to sprout. She prodded one with a finger. "I'm sure they're getting smaller."

The gang stared over at Flicker's wings, wistfully. Every fairy was desperate to get her wings.

"Who do you think will get them first out of us four?" asked Posy.

Rose shrugged. "I don't know," she said. "I'm not even sure what I'm good at yet. At least you know you're good at dancing, Honeysuckle."

"Yes, but—"

The music and singing swelled up again, drowning out their conversation.

"Oi, you little gnats!" shouted Clive from across the pond. "Keep it down! Some of us are trying to sleep!"

Rose grinned at her friends. "Come on," she said, dragging them all up again. "There's plenty of time for wing talk, but not right now. Let's make some noise and annoy some gnomes."

"Too right," said Honeysuckle, and they skipped off to join the dance, whooping and laughing loudly.

Rose gave one last glancc back to the Bigs' house. Sure enough, there at the window was a little girl, her elbows on the windowsill... watching.

Chapter 9

The next morning it was business as usual. The May Day celebrations were over for another year and Mother Nature had returned to Fairyland.

Rose woke up and stretched. Pax was curled up at the end of the bed snoring gently. Rose opened an eye and yawned.

"Morning, you," said Rose sleepily.

Her dragling licked the tip of

her tail then looked confused for a moment, before tucking her head under one wing and going back to sleep again.

Rose looked around the cosy room and contentedly wriggled her toes under her warm blanket. She'd made it out of a fluffy pink sock she'd found in a holly bush. It was as soft as a baby bunny's fur.

Everything in Rose's room was pink. Her four-poster bed was made from pink-headed matchsticks, and had delicate pink lace curtains hung all the way around it. Rose had tied one

of the curtains back with a piece of
Alice's lovely pink ribbon, which she'd
saved from the May Day decorations.

A dolls-house dressing table and
chair sat in one corner of the room, and
a pink crystal chandelier, made from

a lost earring, dangled from the ceiling. Rose had even papered the walls with petals. Pink petals, of course.

On the other side of her door, Rose could already hear the hustle and bustle of morning. She grinned to herself and thought for the zillionth time how much she loved living inside the Fairythorn Tree.

There was a knock on the door and half a second later, Fleur charged in. She was carrying a huge cream envelope that was twice her size. Red shot in after her like a little dragon-shaped cannonball.

"Guess what I've found?" said Fleur, struggling to open the enormous envelope.

"A way to get Derek and Clive to shut up?" asked Rose, grinning.

"I wish," Fleur laughed. "But no. It's much more interesting than that!"

She managed to drag a piece of pink paper out of the envelope. It took up most of Rose's bedroom floor. Rose hopped out of bed.

"What is it?" she asked eagerly.

Just then, Posy and Honeysuckle rushed in through the open door with Dash and Pip hot on their heels.

Honeysuckle stood on the pink paper without realising it, while all the draglings bundled onto the bed on top of Pax.

"Has she read it yet?" Posy asked.

"She will once Honeysuckle gets off it," said Fleur.

Honeysuckle looked down. "Whoops," she said, stepping aside.

"It's a letter to you, Rose," explained Fleur. "I found it stuck to one of the Fairythorn's branches."

Rose knelt down. The paper was covered in neat, purple handwriting. She began to read aloud.

Dear fairy who I saw on the bird,

Hello. You are really pretty. My name is Alice. I am seven and a half. What is your name? Is it true that really important wishes actually do come true?

Me and my mum and my dad have just moved here from the city and I don't know anyone here at all. My mum and dad are always working and I am really lonely. Mum says I will make lots of new friends when I start school after the holidays, but that's ages away!!

Please will you grant my wish for a friend to play with? Thank you.

Alice ♡

P.P. I knew fairies were real. ♡

"Uh-oh, you've definitely been busted," said Posy.

Rose sat back on her heels and nodded. "Looks like it," she said. "I really want to help her, but I don't know what I can do without getting in more trouble."

"It says here, silly," said Honeysuckle. She touched the last line of the letter with a beautifully pointed foot. "Blah, blah, blah… please will you grant my wish for a friend to play with?"

Honeysuckle cartwheeled over the paper. "See? Clear as a raindrop."

Rose sighed. "Do you know how to make a real, live little Big for her to play with then?" she asked.

Honeysuckle stopped doing cartwheels. "I see what you mean," she said.

"I think they're made of guts and bones and stuff," suggested Posy.

"No, that's only the boy ones," said Fleur. "The girl ones are made of sugar and spice."

They all stared in silence at Alice's purple handwriting, thinking hard.

"I have to grant her that wish,"

said Rose finally. "I've just got to figure out how."

Chapter 10

Thoughts of how she might help Alice were bouncing around in Rose's head like fireworks in a tin drum. Her friends had already headed off to start their work for the day, so she decided to go outside and listen to the music of the new morning. Music always calmed her down and helped her to think clearly.

"Come on, Pax," Rose called to her dragling, who scampered up to her and rubbed her furry head against Rose's legs.

She led Pax along the spiralling corridor that sloped its way down through the Fairythorn trunk. Fairythorn trees are a lot bigger inside than they look from the outside, which is just as well, because they have to house an entire community of fairies.

Every available wall and corner had been decorated with shiny things gathered by the fairies while they worked outside in the garden. Doors lined the corridor on both sides. Every now and then one of them would fly open as a fairy dashed out and scurried off to perform their early morning duties.

As Rose passed Flicker's room, the proud Pollen Fairy strode out, nearly slamming her new wings in the door behind her.

"Morning Rose. Going to have to get used to these," she giggled. "That was a close one."

Flicker flapped her butterfly wings proudly behind her. Fairy dust puffed out of them, sparkling like diamonds.

"They're really beautiful," said Rose admiringly.

"Thanks," said Flicker. "Between you and me, though, I feel like I'm carrying a rucksack everywhere. Mother Nature said I won't even notice them in a week, but last night was a nightmare. Every time I rolled over, I knocked everything off my bedside table."

There was a thump behind her closed bedroom door, followed by a sad mewling.

"Dazzling daisies," yelped Flicker, throwing the door open again. "Fizz!"

A black and red dragling shot straight out and leaped into Flicker's outstretched arms.

"Sorry Fizz," she whispered, kissing the top of his head. "I just couldn't wait to get to work today."

Flicker hurried off along the winding corridor. "See you, Rose!" she called out over her shoulder. "Happy sunrise."

Rose broke into a skip and she and Pax soon reached the bottom level of the tree, where they made their way out through the tiny door. They were just in time for the first notes of the dawn chorus. The fairies from the Sunrise Choir lined the branches of the Fairythorn Tree, ready to sing.

A dusting of stars still hung in the sky. The stars glimmered brightly for a moment as the fairies' music began to soar upwards, then faded away as the sun rose over the horizon.

Rose sat on the floor while Pax

chased midges above her head. Rose

sat through the entire sunrise, deep in thought. She was still thinking when the fairy choir had left their branches and gone in for breakfast. But even after all that sitting and thinking she still didn't know what to do.

"Why do Bigs think wishes are so simple to grant?" she muttered to herself. "It's not like the answers grow on trees."

There was a rustle in a nearby bush and a familiar voice came into Rose's head.

"But we have been known to hang answers on bluebell flowers from time to time," the voice said.

Rose was startled, but only for a moment. She knew exactly who the voice belonged to.

Rose knew that Mother Nature was always watching, listening and giving advice when needed. She whispered through the leaves or the long grass on windy days. Or through the babble of a stream or the chatter of bird song… But it was still a surprise to hear her voice out of the blue.

"Good morning, Mother Nature," said Rose. "Um… I'm sorry that I got seen by the little Big… I really really didn't want to break the rules, but I thought a trip to Fairyland would be a worse thing than seeing me."

"Quite right," said the voice.

"Really?" asked Rose, confused. "You're not cross?"

"You listened to your heart," said Mother Nature. "It is a good heart. It will tell you what you need to do if you learn to trust it."

Rose held a hand to her heart. "All mine says is bumpity-bump," she moaned.

The bush rustled as Mother Nature chuckled warmly.

"Look deeper. Listen harder, Rose. You will find the answers." And with a rush of wind and a rustle of leaves, Mother Nature was gone.

Chapter 11

Another busy day in the garden had come to an end. Rose and Posy were moon-bathing. They were stretched out on an old cobweb that hung between the shed and the washing-line post, like a long, thin hammock.

Dash and Pax were splashing around in the pond nearby, driving Derek and Clive mad as usual.

Posy propped herself up on one elbow.

"What was it Mother Nature said, again?" she asked. "Look harder and listen deeper?"

"More or less," grinned Rose. "Look deeper, listen harder."

Posy sighed deeply. "What does that even mean?"

They watched as a shooting star raced across the sky. Being fairies, they could see the hundreds of thousands of wishes following behind the star like a swarm of fireflies.

Rose felt sad to think that Alice's wish was still on her bedroom floor, back at the Fairythorn Tree. But not for long! She was going to make things right.

"It means," Rose said, "that if I keep looking, I will find a way to help Alice." She sat up with a look of determination on her face. "So that's what I'm going to do."

Suddenly, the back door of the Bigs' house swung open and the light from the kitchen poured in to the garden. The biggest Big marched outside, muttering to himself. Rose and Posy scrambled to their feet.

"He's coming this way," yelped Rose, looking about wildly. "We need to get down from here fast. Where are all the sparrows when you need one?"

The long strands of spider web started to bounce alarmingly as the Big stomped across the lawn towards them.

"This way," said Posy, pointing to the washing-line post at one end of the silvery threads.

The fairies hurried as fast as they could along the web, their arms stretched out like tightrope walkers. The Big was coming up fast. In the

darkness, he wouldn't see the cobweb at all.

"He's going to walk straight into us," said Rose.

Posy stuck her fingers in the corner of her mouth and let out a shrill, high whistle. Too high for a Big to hear. A pale-green moth fluttered into sight at once, but seeing the sticky web it paused and backed away, buzzing apologetically.

The Big was only a couple of steps away now.

"There's only one thing for it," said Posy, dropping to a crouch, "Get down and hold tight to the web, Rose."

Rose did as she was told, though she really didn't want to. Posy's plans usually ended badly. The painful kind of badly.

Posy took a deep breath and, pulling a sharp thorn from her pocket, she cut the web.

"What are you doooooooing?"

yelled Rose, as they hurtled through the air like monkeys on a vine.

"I'm saaaaaaaving us!" screamed Posy. "Isn't it oooooooooobvious?"

They swung straight past the Big and crashed against the washing-line post. Rose and Posy clung to the post and watched as the Big flicked on a torch and bustled into the shed. After a few bangs and some loud grumbles, he came out again, carrying a plastic toolbox. Then he marched back up the garden and disappeared into the house.

"Phew," said Rose with relief.

"That was close. Come on. It's a long climb down."

But just then, the kitchen door flew open once more.

Rose frowned. "Oh hang on, it's Alice."

Sure enough, there she was, creeping across the lawn. She flicked on a torch that wasn't as bright as her dad's and made her way towards the Fairythorn Tree.

"What's she doing?" Posy hissed.

They watched as Alice kneeled down at the foot of the Fairythorn. She whispered to the trunk, then placed something on the ground.

Posy and Rose peered hard through the darkness but couldn't quite make the object out.

Then Alice clambered to her feet and ran back to the house.

"Ah, look who's come back for us," said Posy happily. The pale green moth flapped down beside them and the fairies climbed onto his back.

Rose stared up at Alice's window.

"She'll be watching to see if you like the gift she's left," said Posy, looking up too. "It'll be for you, I bet."

Alice's pale face peeked out from behind the curtain then disappeared again.

"If it is," said Rose, "that's two presents and a letter. It's time I got something for her."

Chapter 12

Alice had left Rose a little plastic ring with a sparkly glass gemstone in it.

"It's pink," exclaimed Rose with delight. "How does she know it's my favourite colour?"

"Maybe it's her favourite colour too," Posy suggested.

Pax and Dash fluttered down beside them at the foot of the Fairythorn Tree. The night was very cloudy and every now and again the moon would vanish completely, leaving them in pitch darkness.

"Hello, you two," said Posy warmly. "Been gnome-bothering?"

Dash ran straight over to his mistress and headbutted her. Posy bent down to tickle him under the chin. "Finally driven them mad?"

The draglings purred innocently. Rose ran a hand over the little plastic ring. It was big enough for her to use as a hula hoop.

Alice had left another note and Posy was already busy pulling it out of the envelope. She spread it out on the bumpy ground and began to read.

Hello again fairy,
I forgot to give you a present. My granny
says that fairies like presents so this is
my favourite ring and it is a present for
you. I hope you like it and that giving you
my best most favourite thing will help you
to find me a really good friend. Thanks.
Lots of love from Alice xxxxx

There was a sudden thumping of feet
as two rabbits hopped out of a bush,
followed by a tumbling mess of baby
rabbits.

"Good evening friends," said Rose.

"Hello, fairies," said the mother rabbit. "Sorry about the kids. They're a handful, but we do love them."

"And I love you, Honey-Bunny," said the rabbit dad, snuggling up to his wife.

"Ooo-hoo-hoo, stop it, George," the mother rabbit giggled.

Posy laughed. "How lovely to see such a happy family."

"And to think," said George the rabbit to his wife, "We'd never have met if I hadn't accidentally tunnelled into your living room."

Rose clapped her hands to her mouth. She'd had a brilliant idea. She suddenly knew exactly how to help Alice.

"Thank you! Thank you, rabbits!" she called, grabbing Posy by the hand, "Come on Posy, I've got a plan!"

Chapter 13

Rose spent the next morning dashing about, speaking to every bird, animal and insect she could find. She asked them all to search for little Bigs of Alice's age anywhere in the surrounding streets, then report back.

Rose sat down on a dandelion to wait for news. It would have a pleasant wait, if Alice's mum hadn't decided to try the gnomes in yet another new ~~ ~e garden.

"It's a weapon," Derek was saying.

"Are you stupid as well as ugly?" Clive snorted. "It's quite obviously a comb for an absent giant who will be returning soon."

"Who are you calling stupid, stupid?" snapped Derek. "YOU'RE the stupid one."

Rose rolled her eyes and tried to ignore them.

"It's got all those pokey things on the end," Derek continued. "It's definitely some sort of weapon. If I could move, I'd prove it by clobbering you over the head with it."

"You wouldn't dare!" shrieked Clive.

"Will you two be quiet!" shouted Rose, who couldn't take any more. "It's called a rake. The Bigs use it for gardening," she called over. "It helps them gather up leaves and make seed beds ready for planting."

There was a moment's silence.

"Nah," said Derek.

"Dumb fairy," sneered Clive. "Who asked you, anyway? It's obviously a giant marshmallow fork."

Rose sighed and hopped down

from her dandelion. A squirrel was sprinting towards her, hopefully bringing exciting news.

"She's really pretty," Honeysuckle cooed.

"I love her hair," said Posy.

Fleur burst out laughing. "That's probably because it looks exactly like yours."

Fleur was right. Edie, the little girl that the squirrel had found just half a street away from Alice's house, had the same wild black hair as Posy.

"Maybe," she said, blushing a bit. "But I don't see any feathers in hers."

Rose and her friends were perched on Edie's windowsill, having a good look at her. The curtains were wide open and moonlight filled the room, shining brightly on the face of the sleeping little girl.

An owl hooted politely in a nearby branch. He was waiting to give them a lift home before he caught his dinner. And he was getting hungry.

"Will she do, Rose?" asked Honeysuckle.

They all watched as Edie turned on her side and muttered something into her pillow. There was a hand-made poster above her bed that said, 'NO SMELLY BOYS ALLOWED IN THIS ROOM – BROTHERS ESPECIALLY'.

And lying on the floor next to the bed was a pair of well-worn fairy wings from a dressing-up box. Rose nodded and grinned widely.

"I think she'll be perfect," she said.

Chapter 14

The next day, it was all systems go in Alice's garden. Or, rather, under it. If Alice had stood very still by the garden fence and listened very carefully, she might just have heard the distant thumping, scraping and burrowing of a hundred different animals, deep beneath the shaggy lawn.

After asking Mother Nature's permission, Rose had enlisted all the local burrowing animals for an enormous tunnelling project. When it was finished, the tunnel would lead all the way from Alice's garden to Edie's garden, four doors down the road.

"How long do you think it will take?" asked Honeysuckle, at the end of the first day of digging.

"Three moonrises, maybe four," said Rose with a shrug. "No one quite knows." Her face was covered in mud from the tunnel. As she yawned and stretched, flakes of dried mud dropped from her mucky sleeves.

Rose had been helping with the digging as much as possible and she was exhausted. She couldn't wait to curl up in her bed and close the pink lace curtains around her.

Rose and Honeysuckle climbed the curving slope of the spiral corridor as it wound its way up the trunk of the tree. Pax and Pip trotted along at their mistresses' ankles nipping at each other's wings, playfully.

At night the Fairythorn Tree was a sparkling, busy place, as the Star Fairies came out to work their night shift. The Star Fairies were on the move everywhere, their pale faces smiling and their jet-black wings twinkling with tiny crystals.

There are a great many stars to look after, and without the Star Fairies to tell them what to do, stars have a tendency to bunch up and natter.

"Hello, Lyra. Hello Hydra," said Rose to two Star Fairies who were on their way out.

The Star Fairies tossed their

silver hair and waved happily. Their draglings were also silver, and had a single black star on their foreheads.

"We heard all about your friendship tunnel," said Lyra. "It sounds like a wonderful idea."

"Thanks," said Rose, shyly.

Lyra's dragling, Leo, growled impatiently.

"Come on then, growly," said Lyra. She grinned at Rose and Honeysuckle before marching off briskly. "Sorry, the stars won't wait," she called over her shoulder.

"We'll look out for any shiny

things for you," Hydra promised. "You can use them to decorate the tunnel."

Rose and Honeysuckle continued their climb up the spiral corridor.

"So are the burrowing animals working together well?" asked Honeysuckle.

Rose sighed. "Sort of," she replied. "I mean, the moles seem to think they're in charge, which has put the badgers' noses out of joint a bit. But mostly they're getting on with things."

"Moles can be quite bossy,"

agreed Honeysuckle.

"And," Rose continued, "I had to spend ages cheering up a family of centipedes this morning after one of the moles told them they were too small to help."

Honeysuckle pulled a face. "What a grotmare," she said. But then she smiled brightly. "Lucky you're so nice, Rose," she added. "You're really good at all that stuff."

Rose hadn't really thought about it before. Honeysuckle was right. She really did have a knack for being nice to people and cheering them up.

Suddenly, she felt a tingly sort of an itch on her back. Right between her shoulder blades. Right where her wings would be…

Chapter 15

In the end it took six long, dirty days to build Rose's friendship tunnel. Even the trees had helped by wriggling their roots out of the way.

At Alice's end, the tunnel popped up underneath a huge hydrangea bush. It was completely hidden by the clouds of pink and purple flowers and the lush green leaves. The other end of the tunnel came out under an old iron bench in Edie's garden.

Rose held a small thank-you party, with elderflower fizz and acorn cakes for the animals who had helped. Then, when everyone had wandered back to their burrows and warrens and sets, she sat down under the hydrangeas to go over the last part of her plan.

"Come on, Pax," said Rose. "It's time."

Pax growled excitedly and puffed out a little jet of green fire. They'd been practising all day and Pax was ready for action, but it didn't stop Rose feeling nervous. The wind whispered a warning from Mother Nature to be careful, which did nothing to help her mood at all. She was about to break the Fairy Code and blow her cover again. She knew everything had to go exactly to plan.

At twelve noon sharp, as arranged, Rose and her friends sat waiting on Alice's garden fence. Both little Bigs, according to reports from the squirrels, were in their bedrooms, with their windows open.

A cornflower-blue butterfly flapped down beside Rose and she hopped onto its back.

"Good luck," Honeysuckle said, reaching up to hug her friend.

"Don't get caught. Or squished," said Posy.

Pax took off, then swooped back down to nuzzle into Rose.

"Take care, you," said Rose, hugging her hard.

Rose and the butterfly flew off in one direction and Pax zoomed away in another.

"Right," Rose whispered to the butterfly. "We've only got one shot at this, so let's make it a good one."

The butterfly looped upwards

in a graceful figure-of-eight pattern, then turned hard and went straight for Alice's open window.

Rose looked over her shoulder and caught sight of Pax dipping and bobbing her way over the fences and hedges between Alice and Edie's gardens. Rose felt a strange tugging in her chest as the distance between them grew. Being separated from her dragling felt like being chopped in half. But brave little Pax was obviously concentrating on the job and Rose knew that she must, too. Or all of the animals' hard work on the tunnel would go to waste.

She took a deep breath and hung on tight as they flew over the windowsill and straight into Alice's room.

Chapter 16

Alice was sitting cross-legged on her bed reading. She was so lost in the story that at first she didn't notice the large, cornflower-blue butterfly flapping around her head.

"I know it's a bit rude, but give her a gentle flap in the face," Rose instructed the butterfly. "We need to get her attention."

The butterfly, though, had a better idea and fluttered down to land right on the page of the book that Alice was reading. Rose looked up to see Alice grinning down at her with delight.

"Fairy!" Alice cried. "It's you!"

"Come on, butterfly," shouted Rose, whose voice was too tiny for Alice to hear. She tugged on his feelers and he took off again. "Time to go!"

"No," said Alice, dropping the book and jumping to her feet. "Please don't go. I promise I won't hurt you. Did you like your present?"

"Take us down a bit please," Rose said to the butterfly.

They dropped lower, so that they were at Alice's eye level. The girl's face lit up.

"You're so beautiful," she gasped. Rose beckoned with both hands in a gesture she hoped said 'follow me', then the butterfly turned and flew back out of the bedroom window.

Alice darted out onto the landing and thundered down the stairs. She pushed the back door open and burst outside, shading her eyes with her hands as she peered upwards, searching for the blue butterfly.

"Where are you?" she called out, "Do you want me to follow you?"

Rose and the butterfly flapped down beside her and circled slowly, then led Alice off towards the hydrangea bush.

"What is it?" Alice asked. She watched as the butterfly flew in through a gap between the flowers, then out again, over and over. Rose was standing on the butterfly's back now, waving madly.

"Do you want me to follow?" asked Alice, frowning.

Rose nodded and the butterfly disappeared into the bush again, darting down towards the opening of the tunnel. They hovered there, waiting.

Come on. Rose willed. *Come on, Alice.*

Then sunlight flooded the undergrowth as Alice pushed her way into the bush.

"Wow! A tunnel!" she said, kneeling down and peering in. The opening was as wide as she was and got bigger inside, so Alice could see that there was easily room to crawl.

"Is this where you want me to go, fairy?" asked Alice, spotting Rose hovering in front of her.

Rose nodded again and dived underground.

Alice crawled through the tunnel's entrance. The space inside was lit with little jam-jar lamps, but instead of candles, inside the jam jars were glowing balls of fairy magic.

Alice followed Rose and the cornflower-blue butterfly along the tunnel, gasping at the hundreds of little sparkly decorations set into the walls.

All of a sudden, she heard a voice

deep inside the tunnel. Alice froze.

"Who's there?" Alice whispered.

The voice was getting nearer and louder, but whoever it was hadn't heard Alice at all. They were talking to someone else.

"Hey stop! Please stop!" said the voice. It was getting really close now. "I promise I won't hurt you."

Next thing Alice knew, a little girl came crawling out of the darkness, stopping dead in surprise.

"Whoa!" squeaked Edie. "Where did you come from? Are you like a vampire or something?" she asked.

"Only, I was in my bedroom when a tiny dragon flew in, landed right on my nose and then led me here. So, I'll believe pretty much anything right now."

Alice giggled and shook her head. "No, I'm just a girl," she said. "What about you?"

Edie giggled too. "Same, although my brothers might say different."

"You've got brothers?" Alice said. "You're really lucky."

"You must be joking," Edie replied, grinning. "Brothers are mean and stupid and they smell bad.

I'd much rather have a sister."

Alice had forgotten all about Rose, who was now hiding behind a tree root with Pax and the blue butterfly. As Rose listened to the girls, the itchy feeling tickled at her back again.

"I'm Alice and I live at twenty-six Mulberry Street." said Alice. "Who are you?"

"I'm Edie and I live at thirty-two Mulberry Street," Edie replied. "How come I've never seen you before?"

Alice sat down on a thick, smooth tree root and Edie sat next to her.

"We just moved here," Alice explained.

Rose nudged the butterfly and got ready to leave. It looked like her plan had worked. Now she just needed to sneak off without being seen.

"I know I sound bonkers, but did you happen to see that teeny… um… dragony thing?" Edie asked. "I promise I'm not making it up."

"You mean fairy?" said Alice. "I've seen her too. They're one hundred per cent real."

"It's not a fairy, it's a dragon. It even breathes fire," said Edie.

Alice looked confused.

"It's a fairy all right, I've seen her up close and she's really pretty," she said. "She has beautiful brown hair."

Edie pulled a face.

"Sure, it was cute, but it was covered in green fur!" said Edie.

Rose glanced at Pax and giggled. If Alice and Edie couldn't agree about what they'd seen, none of the other Bigs would ever believe them.

"Come on Pax," she said. "Let's leave them to it."

Rose went to mount the butterfly,

but the tingling on her back stopped her in her tracks. It had grown really hot and itchy all of a sudden. She leaned against the tunnel wall and gasped.

Something was happening. She felt a rush of warmth from her head to her feet and the heat on her back turned to an icy tingle. Then came a sound like a thousand tiny bells ringing…

Chapter 17

"Did you hear that?" said Alice.

The girls turned to follow the sound of bells. Both of their jaws dropped as they spotted Rose, her dragling bouncing up and down excitedly beside her, and her beautiful new wings unfurled. They were a riot of pink and looked just like rose petals. Deeper pink at the tips and paler where they met at her shoulders.

"See!" said Alice. "That's my fairy."

"And that's my dragony thing," said Edie, pointing at Pax, who was tumbling through the air, roaring with delight as she turned a brilliant shade of bright pink.

Rose had a sudden urge to join her. So she did. She bent her knees, pushed hard and soared into the air alongside Pax, whooping loudly. Then she remembered her human audience, and fluttered over to them. She hung in the still air of the tunnel, right in front of their faces. She smiled and held a finger to her lips.

"Promise," said Alice, getting the message right away. "We won't say a thing to anyone. Not even our mums and dads."

"Nor my brothers," said Edie. "Though they'd never believe us anyway," she added.

"And thank you for granting my wish," said Alice. "Thank you for finding me a friend."

Edie patted the walls of the

warm, dry tunnel. "Thanks for the awesome den, too!" she grinned.

Rose curtseyed elegantly in mid-air, then whistled to Pax and shot off towards the surface, flapping her wonderful new wings.

As Rose and Pax flew out of the hydrangea bush, the fairies, who had heard the bells, were waiting with a warm round of applause.

"Over here," Posy shouted. "Hey! Captain Flappy!"

Rose smiled. Her friends were still waiting on the fence for her.

She landed gracefully and closed her wings together. They fluttered about a bit in the afternoon breeze. Clearly they were going to take some getting used to.

"Nice wings," said Fleur, admiringly.

Pax bundled into the other draglings and they licked her new pink fur.

The wind picked up around them and the fairies fell silent. Mother Nature was about to check in.

"Congratulations, Rose," came the familiar voice, carried on the whispering wind. "By finding a friend for Alice, you have also found your purpose and earned your wings. Rose, you are a Wish Fairy."

Rose beamed with joy. She couldn't think of a better job in all the world.

Chapter 18

The draglings were bothering Derek and Clive again. The grumpy gnomes were back by the pond, where Alice's dad liked them, and Pax and Red were dive bombing them with slimy pondweed.

"Clear off!" shrieked Derek, who had so much pondweed on his head that he looked like he was wearing a long green wig.

"Pass me a fly swatter!" moaned

Clive, miserably. "I wish someone would give those draglings a taste of their own medicine. Look out. They're coming back!"

Pax and Red were preparing for another attack. They swooped down together to pick up more slippery weeds, but just as their talons touched the surface of the pond, they crashed into each other, bumping their bony heads and crashing into the murky water.

Moments later they surfaced, spluttering and squeaking, with a thick mass of pond weed tangled

around their legs and wings. They struggled over to the side of the pond and lay there panting.

"Ha!" shrieked Derek. "Classic! Oh, that's made my day, that has. That's made my whole bloomin' year!"

"You see, Derek," said Clive, cackling, "what goes around comes around. As you reap, so shall you sow, and all that."

"Well," muttered Rose to herself from her hiding place on the far side of the pond, "Pax and Red did have it coming. Another wish granted."

She dusted off her hands and wandered away happily, humming to herself. Now that she had earned her wings, she could hardly wait to find out which of her friends would be next.

Say hello to
your new
Fairythorn
friends...

Rose

Rose is kind, sensitive and gentle. She's always trying to make things better for those around her, but is also a worrier. She likes sparkly things, flower petals and weaving decorations into her hair.

Posy

Posy is unstoppable and brave. She adores animals and is often found riding butterflies or chatting to squirrels. Posy loves to wear feathers and her clothes are mainly assembled from things she finds in nature.

Honeysuckle

Honeysuckle is a dreamer. She's a bit dizzy and clumsy, but very sweet with it. She has boundless energy and loves to dance among the flowers, releasing their scent as she pirouettes from bloom to bloom.

Fleur

Fleur is feisty, funny, fiery and cool. Her striking red hair twinkles with tiny stars and her eyes are always changing colour. She loves music and singing. Fleur can make a musical instrument from anything she finds, especially natural things.

Collect them all!

Rose and the
Friendship Wish
ISBN 978-1-84877-968-6

Posy and the
Trouble with Draglings
ISBN 978-1-84877-970-9

Fleur and the
Sunset Chorus
ISBN 978-1-84877-972-3

Honeysuckle
and the Bees
ISBN 978-1-84877-969-3

The Epic Canadian Expedition

Created by Jeff Brown
Written by Sara Pennypacker
Illustrated by Jon Mitchell

EGMONT

EGMONT

We bring stories to life

The Epic Canadian Expedition
First published in the US 2009 as *The Intrepid Canadian Expedition*
First published in Great Britain 2014
by Egmont UK Limited
The Yellow Building, 1 Nicholas Road
London, W11 4AN

Text copyright 2014 by the Trust u/w/o Richard C. Brown
a/k/a Jeff Brown f/b/o Duncan Brown
Illustrations copyright 2014 by the Trust u/w/o Richard C. Brown
a/k/a Jeff Brown f/b/o Duncan Brown

ISBN 978 1 4052 7245 2

1 3 5 7 9 10

Stay safe online. Any website addresses listed in this book are correct at the
time of going to print. However, Egmont is not responsible for content
hosted by third parties. Please be aware that online content can be subject
to change and websites can contain content that is
unsuitable for children. We advise that all children are supervised when
using the internet.

EGMONT LUCKY COIN

Our story began over a century ago, when seventeen-year-old
Egmont Harald Petersen found a coin in the street.

He was on his way to buy a flyswatter, a small hand-operated
printing machine that he then set up in his tiny apartment.

The coin brought him such good luck that today Egmont has
offices in over 30 countries around the world. And that lucky
coin is still kept at the company's head offices in Denmark.

CONTENTS

1.   Stanley Goes Skiing   1
2.   Arthur's Accident   12
3.   Up, Up, and Away!   21
4.   The Northwest Territories   35
5.   Mountie Martin   50
6.   The Stanley Cup   65
7.   Over the Falls!   72
8.   Together Again   78

Chapter One

Stanley Goes Skiing

'Ha, ha!' Arthur Lambchop crowed as he skied past his older brother, Stanley. 'Last one to the bottom is a frozen pancake!'

Stanley grunted as he dug his poles into the snow and strained against the frosty Canadian wind. Ever since he had awakened to find himself flattened by a bulletin board, he'd been putting up with

Arthur's teasing about his shape. He didn't really mind – Arthur was a good brother: cheerful and loyal and a lot of fun.

And so what if being flat made it nearly impossible to ski? It had some mighty big advantages! For instance, he could now travel by mailing himself anywhere in the world for a fraction of the cost of airfare. And he'd sure had a lot of adventures that would not have been available to a rounder boy!

His shape had been a big help to others, also. Stanley allowed himself a little smile of pride as he flapped another few feet down the slope. Wasn't his mother wearing her favourite ring because he had been able to slip down into a storm drain to retrieve it? Wasn't Abraham Lincoln's nose still in place at Mount Rushmore because he had turned himself into a human Band-Aid?

And right now, weren't there a couple of museum sneak thieves playing poker in the city jail who were very sorry indeed they'd ever run into a boy flat enough to pose as a painting?

Just then Arthur whizzed by for a second time. 'See you a-*ROUND*!' he shouted.

Stanley struggled even harder against the wind and reminded himself more firmly he should not feel sad. Why, already on this vacation his flatness had been an advantage: Because he could simply bend his legs at the knees, he had not needed to rent skis. With the money this saved, the Lambchop family had enjoyed a hot-chocolate party in the lodge the night before.

Stanley paused to catch his breath. Really . . . so what if he wasn't aerodynamic any more? The sun was shining on the snowcapped mountains, and the air felt fresh on his cheeks. The scene spread below was straight out of a winter wonderland postcard! Over on the expert trail, daredevils were enjoying the jumps, leaping and twisting in the air. Brightly dressed skiers swooshed by tall, frosted pines.

By the colour of their parkas, Stanley recognised some kids he and Arthur had met the day before. He watched as his brother dashed down to them now, their shouts of greeting drifting up the mountain.

And there, in the middle of the trail, Stanley sank to the snow in defeat.

He couldn't deny it any more: Lately his flatness had made him feel he just didn't have much in common with other people. Lately, it had made him feel lonely.

Tears froze on his eyelashes. He brushed them off to watch Arthur and the other kids weave in and out of each other's paths, gliding gleefully down the mountain. Suddenly, though, Arthur shouted something and broke off from the group. He was heading towards the daredevil skiers!

Stanley scrambled to his feet. 'No, Arthur!' he cried. 'There are jumps!'

Too late! Stanley watched in horror as his brother flew up in the air and then crashed in a pinwheel of skis and poles and flying mittens!

Without a second thought, Stanley angled his body edgewise into the wind, like the blade of a knife. He ripped down the mountain at a terrifying speed, and within seconds he was at his brother's side.

'Are you all right?' Stanley asked. He offered Arthur his hand to help him up.

Just then a boy about Stanley's age skidded to a stop in a spray of snow beside the brothers. 'Don't try to move him!' he warned. 'He may have a broken bone. I'll go to get my father . . . He's a doctor; he's on ski patrol today!' And then, just as suddenly, the boy took off on his snowboard again.

Stanley bent down beside his brother. 'Does it hurt awfully?' he asked. 'Do you

want me to go get Mum and Dad?'

Arthur shook his head. 'Just stay here with me until that fellow's father comes, all right?'

'Of course,' Stanley promised. 'I won't leave you.'

Arthur's Accident

'Ah! Just breathe this fresh Canadian air, Harriet!' marveled George Lambchop to his wife. 'I feel like a new man!'

Before Mrs Lambchop could reply, a boy on a snowboard slooshed to a stop in a cloud of sparkling snow in front of them. 'Are you Arthur and Stanley Lambchop's parents?' the boy asked.

'Oh, dear,' Mrs Lambchop fretted. 'Is everything all right with the boys?'

'Arthur's had an accident. Follow me.'

Mr and Mrs Lambchop hurried to follow the boy.

In the lodge, they were alarmed to see Arthur on a couch, looking quite pale. His ankle was the size of a cantaloupe. A man in a white coat was bending over him, while Stanley looked on anxiously.

'Good gracious!' Mrs Lambchop cried, flying to her son's side. 'Are you all right, dear?'

Arthur winced. 'It hurts a lot,' he admitted. 'But the doctor says it's just a bad sprain.'

At this, the man in the white coat straightened and shook hands with the Lambchops. 'The boy's lucky,' he said. 'He'll have to stay inside and heal for a few days, but then he'll be good as new.'

'Stay *inside*?' Arthur cried. 'No fair! Stanley and I have tickets for the World Snowboarding Championships this afternoon!'

'Out of the question, I'm afraid, young man.' Arthur slumped down with a groan, and the doctor turned back to Mr and Mrs Lambchop. 'I'm Doctor Dave, by the way. It was my boy, Nick, who fetched you.'

'Thank you so much for tending to our son,' Mr Lambchop said. 'Perhaps we should give a call to Doctor Dan, the

boys' regular doctor back home, to let him know what's going on . . .'

'Doctor Dan? Not Doctor Dan of America by any chance?'

When the Lambchops nodded, Doctor Dave smacked his forehead.

'Well, it's a small world indeed!' he exclaimed. 'Doctor Dan and I were roommates in medical school. What a cutup! And he's still got quite a sense of humour. Why, not long ago he wrote to say he was treating a most unusual case – Sudden Flatness Syndrome. As if anyone would believe he'd run into that!'

Doctor Dave chuckled as he packed his bag. Mr and Mrs Lambchop looked at each other in confusion.

'Our son Stanley is –' began Mr Lambchop.

Doctor Dave ignored him and turned to Arthur. 'Remember – complete bed rest, and get lots of exercise. Stay inside and breathe plenty of fresh air. Keep the leg

up, and soak it in ice water – as hot as you can stand it.'

'Hot ice water? Exercise and bed rest? I'm confused!' began Mrs Lambchop.

'Perfectly natural,' Doctor Dave said kindly. 'Don't worry about it. After all, you're not a doctor.'

And then he left.

Stanley couldn't stand to see Arthur looking so glum. 'I'll stay with you,' he said. 'We can play checkers.'

Arthur heaved a big sigh. 'No, you go. One of us might as well be there.' He took a ticket out of his ski pants and held it out. 'And take that boy Nick in my place. To thank him for helping me.'

Stanley was moved by his younger

brother's good sportsmanship. And, as he left to find Nick, he thought maybe this was just the opportunity he needed: Flat or not, he would make a new friend today!

Chapter Three

Up, Up, and Away!

When Stanley and Nick arrived at the course, they noticed that most of the crowd was huddled near the bottom of the run. 'The wind's picked up,' said Nick. 'It'll make for some fantastic boarding. But I wish we could get to the top to watch.'

'Stay behind me,' Stanley told Nick. Then, acting as a windbreak for his new friend, Stanley edged his way up to the start line.

'Thanks!' said Nick. 'We'll have the best view in the place!'

The competition began and Nick was right – the conditions were perfect for some astonishing snowboarding.

'Did you see that fellow? That was an epic jump!' Nick said.

'You sure know a lot about this,' Stanley said admiringly. 'You must be really good.'

'I'm better than good!' Nick bragged. He looked longingly down the trail. 'In fact, if only I had my snowboard, I'd show them a thing or two . . .'

Stanley grinned. 'Well, there are some things I'm really good at, too . . .' Then he stiffened, perfectly straight, with his arms at his side. 'What do you think?'

Nick got the idea at once, but he smirked. 'Are you serious? I only use the best boards! Very expensive . . . like the pros!'

'Oh, come on, let's try it,' Stanley urged.

Nick rolled his eyes. 'All right. Let's go!'

The boys edged their way to a spot alongside the starting gate. Nick pulled on his goggles. 'Ready?'

Stanley lay down in the snow and wrapped his scarf around his middle for foot bindings. 'Ready!'

Nick jumped on top of him, and the starting gun went off. The boys shot down the slope, parallel to the other snowboarders. Nick called out commands, and Stanley positioned himself accordingly.

They made quite a team.

They started on course, weaving through packs of snowboarders as they fired over some moguls. 'Are we in control?' Nick asked.

'I think so,' Stanley replied as they approached a ten-foot kicker jump.

'I hope so!' Nick hollered as they accelerated through the kicker, getting enormous air. The view from thirty feet above the slope was spectacular, peaceful, and still. Stanley caught a snowflake on his

tongue, and then Nick said, 'Stanley, we're going down now!' It was time for the landing, something that neither Nick nor Stanley had considered until that mument. They braced themselves for a rough impact, and were pleased when they glided gently into some thick powder, skidding away in a wake of snow. 'That wasn't so bad,' Stanley reflected.

'Stanley! Stanley!' Nick was pointing ahead, trying his best to keep Stanley on course as they veered off the trail and into the woods!

'Look, a jib!' Nick said. He guided them towards a fallen tree where snowboarders were sliding over the trunk. They glided up and over the length of the log, spinning as onlookers admired their flair. 'Wheeeeee!' Stanley and Nick shouted together. They landed and sped back to the course, going faster than ever.

'Ladies and gentlemen, it seems we have a new challenger!' shouted the sports announcer. 'And he's giving the professionals some competition!'

The wind blew even stronger now. 'I'm going to cut you into it now,' Nick told Stanley. 'If we can catch a current, I bet we can kill it!'

'Are you sure?' called out Stanley. 'We're going higher than anyone else already!'

'That's just where I *should* be!' yelled Nick. 'Bombs away!'

Stanley strained upwards to catch the wind, remembering what he'd learned when Arthur had flown him like a kite. Up and up he went, while Nick crouched to hold on to Stanley with one hand. The crowd below roared in delight. Even the other snowboarders, finished with the run now, cheered in awe.

Stanley realised the problem first. 'I can't come down!' he yelled to Nick. 'I've caught the current, and I can't get out of it!'

Nick shouted, 'No way, dude! I've got it under control.' He tried to guide the Stanley-board down, but it was no use . . . Suddenly, an even stronger gust of wind flipped them completely over. 'Grab my hands and feet!' Stanley called to Nick.

Nick did, just in time, and Stanley allowed himself to billow in the wind like a parasail. The boys floated even higher over the course.

Far down below in the crowd, Stanley caught sight of his father, standing with Doctor Dave, looking very worried.

'We're going to fall!' Nick screamed.

Both fathers gestured wildly with puzzled looks.

'No, we're not,' Stanley tried to assure

Nick. 'Just don't let go!'

But Nick was panicking. 'We're going to fall!' he screamed even louder down to the dads. *'We're going to fall!'*

'No, not unless the wind were to stop all of a sudden,' Stanley told Nick. 'I'm not shaped for skiing any more, but I'm just right for riding the air currents. Just hold on tight until the wind dies down, all right?'

Nick remained nervous, but he held tight. Up so high it was curiously quiet, in spite of the wind. Stanley decided to take Nick's mind off the situation by chatting. 'My family is going to a wedding next week. It's somewhere near the Canadian border, so we decided to get a ski vacation in before it.'

'That's nothing,' Nick said. 'I'm the ring bearer for a wedding next week!'

'We had a hot-chocolate party at the

lodge last night,' Stanley tried.

'I drank four mugs yesterday,' said Nick. 'With extra marshmallows!'

'Then we watched a good show – about the Royal Canadian Mounted Police.'

'I've seen every episode,' Nick bragged.

No matter what Stanley mentioned, Nick had done it better, faster, or more times.

Stanley began to feel a little discouraged, but he kept talking all afternoon because it was working – Nick was relaxing.

As the sky darkened, the two boys grew tired. 'You sleep a little first,' Stanley offered. 'One of us should always stay awake in case we come down.'

Stanley steered them over the darkening

mountains for a few hours as Nick dozed, then when the moon had risen, Nick awoke and let Stanley close his eyes.

Stanley would have preferred to have his pillow and warm blankets at the lodge, with his brother in the next bed. But within minutes, he was sound asleep.

The Northwest Territories

Stanley awoke to a poke in the ribs. The sun was shining brightly, and the wind had nearly stopped.

'We're coming down!' Nick shouted. 'Fast!'

Stanley looked down . . . Nick was right! They were hurtling towards a frozen landscape at a dangerous speed.

'Three, two, one . . . Roll!' Stanley cried. He arched his back even more – like a parachute – and they crashed softly to the ground, tumbling head over heels through snow and brush.

When they gathered themselves enough to sit up, they were stunned to find a man in a huge fur collar towering over them. 'An *Eskimo*!' Nick breathed.

'That's *Inuit*,' the man corrected him, smiling. 'We're native people. I am Tulugaq.' He extended one hand to each boy and pulled them to their feet easily. Beside them, a furry dog was yapping and dancing around.

'This is Amarok. It means "wolf", but he's very friendly. He watched you fall

from the sky . . . He's never seen birds as big as you!'

Nick straightened up. 'I'm bigger than he is!'

Tulugaq frowned a little. 'Well, no matter, you both look half frozen – follow me.'

Nick and Stanley followed the Inuit man across the frozen tundra and into a little wooden house.

'You don't live in an igloo?' Nick asked.

Tulugaq rolled his eyes and laughed a hearty laugh. 'There is a lot you don't know about my culture,' the man said. 'Come inside and you will see that we are very modern.'

Inside the house, Stanley and Nick were grateful to warm themselves by a roaring fire. Tulugaq introduced the boys to his wife, his grandmother, and half a dozen cheeky children who were scampering about, passing around bowls of caribou stew.

The boys ate as Tulugaq told stories about his people. Then, everyone was eager to hear the story of how Nick and Stanley had arrived.

'You travelled so far!' Tulugaq's grandmother marveled. 'You floated right over the Rocky Mountains and into the Northwest Territories!'

'I steered,' boasted Nick.

Tulugaq's wife patted Stanley's hand.

'Your family must be very worried. Here, use our phone to call them, to let them know you are safe.'

Stanley called the ski resort, eager to
hear his parents' voices and to tell Arthur
all about his adventure. 'I'm sorry,' the

receptionist said. 'The Lambchop family checked out yesterday.'

Nick grabbed the phone. 'How about my family? Connect me to Doctor Dave's room – it's the VIP suite!'

'Sorry,' said the receptionist. 'Doctor Dave and his party checked out yesterday also.'

Stanley and Nick were too stunned to speak.

Tulugaq turned to his wife and said something in Inuit. Then he put his hand on Stanley's shoulder.

'We must visit the shaman now,' said Tulugaq. 'Come.'

Stanley and Nick left with Tulugaq, still quite upset. Why would their families have

left without them? And where could they have gone?

'The shaman is wise,' Tulugaq told them as they travelled across the village. 'He will have an answer.'

But Nick and Stanley were not reassured. In fact, they were so worried, they barely even noticed that they travelled over a frozen river on a bridge of ice. *Where were their families?*

At last they came to a small, ancient hut. Tulugaq ducked inside and waved for the boys to follow him. In the dim light from an oil lamp, the boys could see that the walls were hung with animal furs and weavings and ancient artifacts.

Suddenly, one of the furs – huge, and with a monstrous mask on top – leaped to life and came straight for them!

The monster pulled off his mask to reveal . . . a very tiny, very wrinkled old Inuit man. He hugged Tulugaq and the two spoke for a mument in their language. Then Tulugaq pointed to the boys and the old shaman turned. His eyes widened when he saw Stanley's shape. He walked all around him, eyeing him closely from all angles. The shaman seemed so impressed and respectful that Stanley didn't feel a bit embarrassed by all the curiosity.

Next the shaman handed a skin drum to Tulugaq. Tulugaq began to beat it, and the shaman began to chant and dance around the room. Faster and faster he whirled, almost as if he was in a trance.

Finally he spun to a stop and seemed to come back to himself. He smiled broadly, without a tooth in his head, and said something to Tulugaq.

'He says you boys are going to make a great journey together,' Tulugaq translated. 'You will go to the great falling waters.

There, something will happen that will bond you to each other for life. Like brothers!'

'The great falling waters?' asked Nick. 'Where's that?'

The shaman reached into a pouch he wore around his neck and pulled out a worn and creased postcard. He showed it to the boys.

'Niagara Falls!' Stanley cried. 'I've heard of that! But how far away is it?'

'Near Toronto, in Ontario. Many miles away,' answered Tulugaq. 'Thousands. Canada is a very large country.'

Stanley and Nick exchanged looks – two boys on foot with no money could never travel that far.

Later that night, after a satisfying meal of dried fish and boiled walrus, the boys sat on the steps outside Tulugaq's home.

'Normally, I would just mail myself home,' Stanley said. 'But I don't think I should leave you here.'

Nick nodded. 'Besides,' he said, 'we don't know that there'd be anyone at our homes when we got there.'

'I don't know what to do,' Stanley said. 'The shaman said we were supposed to make the journey together. Tulugaq says there's a dog sled to Calgary, where his cousin lives, but that's just a short part of the trip . . .'

Both boys fell silent then, looking down at the frozen ground, discouraged.

After a while, though, Stanley – not being the kind of boy to give in to discouragement – looked up.

And then he gasped in disbelief! The night sky was shimmering with iridescent lights – neon greens and pinks and yellows danced across the entire horizon!

'The northern lights, Nick!' Stanley said

at last. 'It's a sign. If the whole sky can light up like that, I guess you and I can make our way to Niagara Falls somehow!'

Nick and Stanley shook hands. 'We'll do it,' they declared. 'Like brothers!'

Mountie Martin

The next morning Stanley and Nick said good-bye to their hosts and found the dog sled team in the village. There was only one seat left, so Stanley gamely volunteered to ride, under everyone's feet. The ride was bumpy, but every time he was tempted to complain, Stanley recalled the magical sky he and Nick had seen.

At last they arrived at the city of Calgary. The dog sled driver dropped them off at the address Tulugaq had provided. Stanley and Nick knocked.

When the door opened, Nick cried out, 'This must be the wrong address! We're looking for Tulugaq's cousin.'

'Cousin Tulugaq sent you? Well, come on in, little pardners! This is the spot all right!'

'But how come you're not . . . How come you look like a cowboy?' Nick demanded – a little rudely, it must be said.

'And native people can't be cowboys, is that it? Well, guess again, little pardner. This is Calgary, the Wild West of Canada. I'm Nauja and I'm Inuit . . . and I'm also a

cowboy! Now come on in from the cold
and meet my family!'

'I guess I shouldn't have been surprised
that a cousin of Tulugaq would be a
cowboy,' Stanley said thoughtfully after

he'd been introduced to Nauja's wife and children. 'A girl I met at Mount Rushmore – Calamity Jasper – taught me that anyone can be a cowboy. She was part Lakota Sioux.'

A smile came to Stanley's face as he remembered her. 'She taught me some other things, too,' he said. 'Do you have a rope I could borrow?'

Nauja brought a length of rope, and then Stanley entertained everyone with lariat tricks the cowgirl had shown him.

Nick sat in a corner, scowling. 'Nobody likes a show-off, you know!' he muttered.

Just then a knock came at the door. There on the steps stood a man wearing a bright red coat, a big tan hat, and tall

brown boots. He towered over everyone, so straight and powerful-looking, Stanley wondered for a minute if he was real.

Nauja gave the man a big bear hug. 'Mountie Martin! What are you doing here, so far from Quebec?'

'Working. My partner and I chased a dangerous desperado out here. I figure . . . I'm so close to *mon cher* cousin I might as well stop by for a quick visit . . . *non*?'

'You're Nauja's cousin, too? And Tulugaq's?' asked Nick.

'*Oui*. The French–Canadian side of the family, by marriage. Mountie Martin, at your service,' he saluted to the boys. 'And who might you be?'

The boys introduced themselves and explained they were trying to get to Niagara Falls. Then Stanley asked what he was dying to know. 'That dangerous desperado you were chasing . . . did you get him?'

The Mountie beamed. 'But of course I

got him, *mon ami*!' he cried. 'I am a Royal Canadian Mounted Police officer. We always get our man! Now, how would you fellows like a ride to Quebec? My partner had to fly back with the desperado, and I could use the company. I could get you a lot closer to Niagara Falls.'

Nick and Stanley made their good-byes and got into Mountie Martin's cruiser. The Mountie made adjustments to Stanley's seat belt until it held him snugly. 'Safety first, *eh*? No matter the shape!'

Mountie Martin insisted they begin the trip with a big meal of Canadian specialties. 'My treat,' he said. 'The United States of America is our neighbour. I am just being neighbourly while you are visiting us!'

The boys – having the healthy appetites that travel brings on – enjoyed everything. Stanley's favourite was *poutine*. 'French fries with cheese and gravy . . . what could be better?' he asked.

'Maple taffy,' answered Nick. He poured more hot syrup over snow for a second helping of the sticky dessert.

Back on the road, Mountie Martin was a good guide. He pointed out mountains, rivers, and cities as they covered the vast and beautiful lands of Canada. All the sights reminded him of a story or an interesting bit of history. Whatever he said, Nick seemed to already know about it.

On the second day, the conversation turned to sports. 'Canada was a good choice for the 2010 Olympic Games,' Mountie Martin said. 'We are a nation of winter-sports lovers!'

At that, Nick listed all his favourites: skiing, skating, luging, and snowboarding. Nick was an expert at everything. Stanley slid down in his seat and stared out the window. At least, he thought, at least with every minute we are getting closer to Niagara Falls. And closer to home . . .

'How about you, Stanley?' Mountie Martin interrupted his thoughts. 'Who's your favourite team?'

'Excuse me?'

'We were talking about hockey. Here in Canada, it is our national sport – the greatest sport in the history of the world!'

Stanley slid even farther down in his seat. 'I've never seen a game,' he mumbled, almost to himself.

'I'm a huge fan!' Nick exclaimed. 'I've been to lots of games!'

Mountie Martin braked abruptly – but with caution and complete control. He pulled the cruiser over to the shoulder of the road and snapped the flashing lights on. 'Safety first,' he explained. 'Now, would you please say that again, young man?'

Nick beamed. 'I said I've been to lots of hockey games – I'm the biggest fan!'

'No, not you,' the Mountie said. He nodded to Stanley. 'You, *mon ami*. What did you just say?'

Stanley felt himself blush with embarrassment. 'I've never been to a hockey game,' he admitted.

'Well,' said the Mountie, 'here in Canada, that is a very serious offense – a crime! And since I am a sworn officer of the law, I cannot let this crime continue. I'm afraid I'm going to have to arrest you and take you to a . . .'

Stanley gulped, waiting for his punishment.

' . . . A hockey game!' Although Mountie Martin said this in a stern voice, he wore a big smile.

In the backseat, Stanley grinned and saluted. 'Yes, sir, Mountie Martin, sir! I'm sorry for breaking the law!'

'No fair!' cried Nick. 'I'm a bigger fan than he is!'

Mountie Martin turned to face Nick. 'A team that competes with itself is not a very strong team. You understand? *Oui?*'

'We?' Nick asked. 'You mean Stanley and me, do *we* understand?'

'No,' Mountie Martin began. '*Oui* means "yes", in French. But *oui*, I do mean you and Stanley. Look: You tell me stories about snowboarding as a pair, travelling across Canada together, flying through the air, relying upon each other. You make your way back across this whole country – again, because you are a team. Why must you always compete? In the Royal Canadian Mounted Police, we learn to rely on our partners. We must always be *WE*. Now if you are ready to be a real team, I think I will take you *both* to this hockey game tonight!'

'Sure. For a hockey game, we'll be a team!' Nick smiled, but Stanley noticed he had crossed his fingers.

The Stanley Cup!

That night, as promised, Mountie Martin stopped in Ottawa and took the boys to a hockey game. 'The Maple Leafs are playing. They're my favourite team, even though I am from Quebec,' he admitted.

The game was as thrilling as Stanley had always heard. At half time, a contest was announced. The fan with the best sign would be invited down to the ice and given one chance to score a goal. If the fan made the shot – a one-in-a-hundred chance – he or she would win a trip to the Maple Leafs' next game, which was in Toronto.

Toronto! Stanley looked around at the packed stadium. Hundreds of fans were waving signs. Suddenly he had a terrific idea. 'Do you think you can hold me up if I stand on your shoulders?' he asked Nick.

Nick flexed his muscles. 'Of course! I'm probably the strongest kid here!' He caught Mountie Martin's warning look, and then he said, 'Well, you're pretty strong, too, Stanley.' He made a step out of his hands. 'Here, I'll give you a boost.'

'Not yet,' said Stanley. He pulled his red scarf way down over his face and pulled his red turtleneck up to meet it. And then to Nick and Mountie Martin's amazement, he folded his upper body into a perfect maple leaf. He pleated his legs, in their brown pants, into a stem! 'I learned origami while I was in Japan not long ago,' came Stanley's muffled voice from somewhere inside the leaf. 'Now hoist me up, Nick!'

Nick did, and the crowd went wild.

'There's our winner!' shouted the announcer. 'No question at all! Come on down to the ice!'

Nick, holding the Stanley-maple leaf up in triumph, made his way down to the

rink, surrounded by the admiring crowd. When he reached the centreline, Stanley jumped from his shoulder and unfurled himself. And the fans went wild.

When the applause finally died down, the captain of the Maple Leafs skated over and handed Nick a puck and a hockey stick.

Stanley whispered something to Nick. Then Nick handed the puck back to the team captain. 'No thanks,' he said. 'We'll use our own!'

And then Stanley lay down on the ice and coiled himself into a tight disk. Nick took aim and swung the hockey stick hard, whacking Stanley on the soles of his boots. Stanley skittered crazily across the ice. He was hurtling for the side line – nowhere near the goal. Stanley quickly calculated the angle and adjusted himself. When he hit the boards, he ricocheted off, now aiming right for the ...

'Goal!' yelled the announcer. 'I don't believe my eyes, but these two boys from America have just done the impossible!'

'You did the impossible, Stanley,' Nick said when Stanley uncoiled himself. 'Mountie Martin was right . . . We really do make a good team!'

The captain of the team skated over and shook both the boys' hands. He handed them the box seat tickets and airline tickets. 'See you in Toronto!' he said.

Over the Falls!

The next morning, bright and early, Stanley and Nick said good-bye to Mountie Martin at the airport and boarded the plane. 'Whatever happens at Niagara Falls,' they told each other, 'we're already like brothers.'

The flight was pleasant, but with nothing to distract them, both boys began to worry about their families again. Where had they gone? How would they ever be reunited again?

By the time they landed, Stanley and Nick were very homesick indeed.

An airport shuttle bus whisked them to Niagara Falls. As soon as they stepped off the bus, they heard the powerful waterfalls crashing in the distance. They couldn't see anything except a great cloud of misty spray, though. They headed for the sound, along with a crush of tourists.

As they walked, they passed several signs. 'Look, Nick,' Stanley pointed one out. 'The falls are more than one hundred and seventy feet high here.'

'One hundred and fifty thousand gallons

of water goes over the crest line every second,' Nick read on another.

Just then the mist cleared. The boys stared in wonder at the majestic sight of Niagara Falls, thundering beside them in a curtain of rainbows.

Nick ran to the railing. 'Come here, Stanley!' he cried over the roar. 'It's awesome!'

Stanley rushed to catch up. But when he reached the edge, he began to flap in the winds churned up by the rushing water. How could he have forgotten his problems with wind so soon?

A sudden gust lifted him and plastered him to a signpost dangerously close to the edge. Stanley tried to slither down, but the wind held him tight.

Nick climbed up on to the rail to try to peel him off. 'You're the first friend I've ever had,' he cried. 'The only one who's put up with my bragging. I'm not about to lose you now!'

But as he struggled to push Stanley down to safely, Nick lost his footing on the mist-slicked metal. Over the railing he went, hurtling through the air, straight for the crashing waterfalls below!

Stanley didn't think for a second. He launched himself out, reached Nick in midair, and curved himself around his new friend. Like a barrel!

Together they crashed to the churning water. Over and over and over they

smashed and battered against the rocks
and angry waters.

Finally, the terrible tumbling stopped,
and all was still blackness.

Together Again

Stanley awoke to find his parents' faces hovering above him. He rubbed his eyes ... Was this a dream? Or worse – was he ... dead?

'My goodness, dear, you gave us quite a fright!' said his mother.

'Mum! Dad! What are you doing here?' Stanley asked.

'Don't you remember?' Mr Lambchop asked. 'When you were up so high at the snowboarding championships, you kept yelling, "We're going to the Falls! We're going to the Falls!" We would never have allowed it if we'd known you were planning to go *into* the falls, though! We just thought you'd meet us here for the wedding.'

'What? No, that was Nick. He was yelling . . . oh, never mind. The important thing is that you're here! I'm so glad to see you! But, hey, where *is* Nick?'

'Hay is for horses, dear,' Mrs Lambchop reminded him. 'Do try to remember that. Nick is over there. His father is examining him now.'

Doctor Dave came over then. 'My boy's fine,' he said. 'How about I take a look at yours, Lambchops?'

'Please do!' said Mr and Mrs Lambchop at the same time.

Doctor Dave gave Stanley a thorough examination. Then he called Stanley's parents back over. 'No broken bones, that's the good news,' he began.

'Oh, dear!' Mrs Lambchop exclaimed. 'If there's bad news, you'd better give it to us right away. Delaying it won't make it any easier.' Harriet Lambchop was both very practical and very brave.

'Well, here it is, then,' Doctor Dave said. 'The repeated violent impact with the rushing water has flattened your son. Water trauma can do that. That's why you don't see anyone swimming around here. I can't tell how long the flatness will last, but you should be prepared for the worst.'

'But, Doctor Dave, Stanley was flat before all this,' Mrs Lambchop said. 'So if that's all, then he's fine!'

Doctor Dave patted Mrs Lambchop's hand. 'Denial. Very common in cases like this. You just keep thinking whatever you need to think in order to get through it. Well, I must be off . . . Nick and I have a wedding to get to.'

'Why, so do we!' Mrs Lambchop said. 'I know a lot of people get married at Niagara Falls, but do you suppose it's the same wedding?'

Wonder of wonders, it was! The bride was an old college chum of Nick's mother, Shelby Smith. The groom was an old college chum of Stanley's father, Ralph Jones. Their families sat on different sides of the aisle, but Stanley watched with pride as his new friend, Nick, carried the ring for the bride and groom.

Afterwards, at the reception, Stanley,

Nick, and Arthur had a wonderful time together. Doctor Dave had been right about Arthur's ankle – a few days of rest and it was as good as new.

After a while, Mr and Mrs Lambchop came over to fetch the boys. 'It's time we congratulated the newlyweds.'

As they walked over, Stanley told Nick about the groom. 'Mr Jones has a remarkable memory . . . He never forgets anything!'

And sure enough, when they reached Mr Jones, he astonished them with his perfect recall. 'Hello there, Stanley,' he said. 'What do you hear from Egypt? That Sir Abu Shenti Hawara the fourth still in prison for trying to rob the tomb of

Pharoah Khufufull?'

Mr Lambchop came up then. 'Congratulations, Ralph,' he said, shaking his friend's hand. 'That wonderful memory of yours should make for a happy marriage, I predict. At least you'll never forget your anniversary!'

'Let's hope so,' Ralph Jones said. 'But, you know, my excellent memory is the very thing that kept me from marrying Shelby years ago.' Here he paused to gaze down at his bride fondly. 'All this time apart . . . what a waste!' He sighed.

'What happened?' Stanley asked.

'We went to high school together. I remembered that once, at a football game, Shelby had smiled fetchingly at the star quarterback. His name was B.F. Wellington. Big fellow. Everyone called him Beef. Beef Wellington . . . get it? Har, har. Except my heart was broken . . . Shelby had smiled at him, not me. For all these years, Shelby denied it. But then finally, she admitted she *had* smiled at him . . . but only to make me jealous. So I forgave her and asked her to be my bride.'

The new Mr and Mrs Jones kissed each other then.

'In a marriage,' Mrs Lambchop advised the groom, 'forgiveness is much more important than memory.'

'That sounds like good advice,' Mr Jones said. 'I'll try to remember that.'

That evening, the Lambchops enjoyed the Maple Leafs' game very much. But all four of them agreed they were even happier to return home that evening.

Stanley thumbtacked a newspaper clipping to the bulletin board over his bed. The headline read:

'That was quite a vacation,' Stanley said. 'I wish you could have made the trip with me, though, Arthur.'

'It was my fault,' Arthur said. 'I was showing off on the ski slope. And Stanley . . . I'm sorry for all the teasing about your shape.'

'That's all right,' Stanley replied. 'Actually, it's kind of *flat*-tering.'

He turned off the lamp, and the two brothers lay in their beds chuckling for a few minutes about Stanley's joke. And then they fell fast asleep.

EGMONT PRESS: ETHICAL PUBLISHING

Egmont Press is about turning writers into successful authors and children into passionate readers – producing books that enrich and entertain. As a responsible children's publisher, we go even further, considering the world in which our consumers are growing up.

Safety First
Naturally, all of our books meet legal safety requirements. But we go further than this; every book with play value is tested to the highest standards – if it fails, it's back to the drawing-board.

Made Fairly
We are working to ensure that the workers involved in our supply chain – the people that make our books – are treated with fairness and respect.

Responsible Forestry
We are committed to ensuring all our papers come from environmentally and socially responsible forest sources.

**For more information, please visit our website at
www.egmont.co.uk/ethical**